# All About Bikes

Annette Smith

## Contents

Bikes Are Vehicles ............................................. 2

Bikes for Everyone ........................................... 8

Mountain Bikes .................................................. 12

BMX Bikes ........................................................... 14

Glossary ............................................................... 16

# Bikes Are Vehicles

People ride bikes so they can go quickly from one place to another.

People ride bikes on roads in a city or on paths in the country.

All bikes have wheels.
Most bikes have two wheels.
The wheels are fixed to a **frame**.
One wheel is in front of the other.

The bike rider sits on a seat
and holds the handle bars to steer the bike.

Then, the rider moves the bike
by pushing down on two **pedals**.
There is a long **chain**
from the pedals to the back wheel.
The chain makes the wheel turn.

A long time ago, bikes had a big wheel
at the front and a small wheel at the back.
The rider sat on a seat
that was high off the ground.
The rider had to be very careful not to fall off.

Sometimes, clowns ride one-wheel bikes
in a street parade or at a fair.
These clowns have to be clever
to ride this kind of bike.

# Bikes for Everyone

Children who are learning to ride
can have training wheels.
These wheels are very small.
They are fixed to the back wheel of the bike.
Children do not fall off bikes
with training wheels.

As children get older,
they soon begin to ride bigger bikes.

These bikes go much faster
than the bikes with training wheels.
Children can learn to ride the bigger bikes
on the grass in their backyards
or on the paths at a park.

Children have to practise
how to get on and off their bikes safely.

Some people ride bikes to work.
They leave their cars at home.

Other people ride bikes to keep fit.
On Saturdays and Sundays,
they will often go for long rides
out into the country with their friends.
Sometimes, they have races to another town.

# Mountain Bikes

Mountain bikes have bigger **tyres** than road bikes.
The bigger tyres are better for riding along muddy tracks in forests.

Mountain bikes have more gears, too.
The riders put their bikes into low gears
when they go up steep hills.

They always ride carefully
as they go over rocks and through streams.

# BMX Bikes

BMX bikes are racing bikes.
They have strong frames so they don't break
when the rider hits a bump on the track.
BMX bikes have small wheels.
The small wheels are quick to turn.

The riders do tricks and high jumps
in the air on their bikes.

Today, many people ride bikes for fun and to keep fit.

# Glossary

**chain**     a string made of links

**frame**     the main part of the bike

**pedals**     steps on a bike that are moved by pushing on them with your feet

**tyres**     the outer parts of the wheels that go on the road